THE RECIPE OF A
Godly Woman

THE RECIPE OF A
Godly Woman

LATOYA GETER-SHOCKLEY

LITTLE ROCK, ARKANSAS

The Recipe of a Godly Woman
Copyright 2018 by Latoya Geter-Shockley

J. Kenkade Publishing
6104 Forbing Rd
Little Rock, AR 72209
www.jkenkade.com
Facebook.com/jkenkadepublishing

J. Kenkade Publishing is a registered trademark.
Printed in the United States of America

ISBN 978-1-944486-70-9

This is a work of fiction. Names, characters, businesses, places, events and incidents are either the products of the author's imagination or used in a fictitious manner. Any resemblance to actual persons, living or dead, or actual events is purely coincidental. The views expressed in this book are those of the author and do not necessarily re-flect the views of Publisher.

Dedicated to my late mother, Romunda Owens
and my grandmother, Betty Williams

Lauren

M y hometown of Crestview was small with two sides. The east and the west. The town hall sat right in the middle separating the two sides. They were definitely different. The east was home to the rich uppity. You know the lawyers, doctors, politicians and entrepreneurs. The west was home to many drug dealers, the homeless, prostitutes and trying individuals. The population was 1,000. The members of my childhood church on the east side of town, Temple of Heaven were preparing for our evening service to welcome our new pastor. The pastor's committee, myself, Allison, Kim and Tamika were in charge of the program. We decorated the sanctuary before the service started.

"Looks good in here Ladies," said Tamika.

"I'm about to go make sure the office for our new pastor is nice!"

I watched as Kim eyed her. I knew she was about to comment and so she did, by mocking Tamika,

"Go make sure his office is nice!"

"Don't start" I begged her.

"Please don't" pleaded Allison. We both knew Kim was that church member that said whatever came to her mind. So of course, she went on and on.

"She's going to be after the new pastor. He has no first family! No first lady!"

I couldn't help but to add my two cents, "He is handsome too."

Kim shook her head, "She is gone be on him like red ink in the book of Matthew!"

"Stop it" laughed Allison.

"I hope he doesn't fall for her, if those are her intentions," I sighed.

"You know the town is small and it's not many single women" said Allison, "He just might!"

"Well, we are going to pray he doesn't," laughed Kim.

Residents of the town and other churches

came to the welcome service. The sanctuary was filling as the committee lined the pews to begin the service. We looked for Tamika, but we could not find her. We then saw her stand in the doorway of the sanctuary. She had the nerve to be his escort. The committee didn't agree on that. She even wore the same purple flower he wore, both on their right side.

Kim whispered to us, "I told yall."

I had to admit, he was handsome, just like I remembered him to be from visiting in the past. He was two seconds from being 6 feet tall. A vanilla with a swirl of chocolate ice cream cone that any woman would die to be the cherry on top of. Brown hazelnut eyes that made you want to take an extra lick, I mean bite and I just wanted to run my hands down his brown wavy hair cut while he slept on my stomach.

Pastor Reynolds

❧

I was the new pastor of Temple of Heaven. I was not a resident of Crestview, but I had been to visit before. Things were still new to me. After the welcome service, the next day, I went by the church. I wanted to become familiar with things. I knew the church clerk would be there. She could help me out.

"Good morning," I said stepping into her office, "I was wondering if you had time to show me around."

"Good morning Pastor. Yes, I can take you around" she smiled.

I noticed her outfit. It was rather revealing. I tried not to stare too much, but it was very noticeable. The skirt fit every curve of her lower body. The blazer was so tight that her cleavage was almost spilling into my grasp. The devil!

"You weren't too busy, were you?" I asked, trying to rebuke the work of Satan.

"No, I wasn't," she smiled.

She then had the nerve to switch past me!

Was she doing that on purpose? Did she think I was staring at her intentionally? I was not! Her clothes were just that revealing.

After showing me around the church, we ended back at the offices.

She yawned as we stopped. "Long day," I said.

"Long night," she added. "I work as a nurse at the hospital at night. Then I come here. 8:00 p.m. – 4:00 a.m."

"God bless you sister," I said. "Do you need to go home and rest?"

She assured me she was fine and asked if I needed anything else. There was one more thing I needed her to do.

"Can you please call all committee chairs. I would like to have a mass meeting with them next Saturday in the sanctuary at 2:30 p.m."

"I will get that done!" she smiled.

She did get the job done just as she said

she would. I met with the committee members of the church to share an idea of bringing the town together. I was willing to hear their ideas as well. After all, it was their community. My plan was to reach out to the children at the local schools through after school programs or field trips. Friendships would develop and hopefully the children would grow into adults that would mingle on both sides of the town ending the segregated mentality. There was no need to try to bring stubborn adults that were stuck in their ways together. They would not see the vision! The church members actually agreed to help with the idea, but there were some that did not believe the parents would be on board, but we still stuck to the plan. We reached out to local schools that were willing to participate from both sides. Two elementary schools from each side decided to join the effort! That was better than none.

Our first trip to a zoo located outside of the town was a success!

Twenty youth attended and they all received a sponsored shirt to make them feel equal. I watched as they laughed and played together! The vision was starting but I knew it was far from being complete.

I had been in Crestview for three months and unlike other residents on the east side, I would visit the west side. There was a café there that served pretty darn good breakfast. I had to stop by every morning! I was a regular. Employees treated me nicely! The chef knew what I loved!

Audrey

❦

My little sister was not feeling well. So, she asked me to go to work at the café for her. I was tired from my second job, but we could not afford for my sister to lose the job. That meant I had to work her shift and my shift at the café plus go to my second job. I was going to be one tired sister! She couldn't babysit Ariel, my 4-year-old daughter. I had to take her to the café with me. She loved going! Our boss didn't mind. She wasn't any trouble. We walked into the café and my baby eyes lit up like it was Christmas. She took off toward this man sitting in a booth eating breakfast. I thought it was her dead-beat dad-dy, but there was no way he would be dressed in black dress pants, with a navy-blue dress shirt and light tie to match!

"Pastor R!" she yelled out. I watched as he stood up and they hugged. I then realized who he was.

"So, you're pastor Reynolds. Hi, I'm Ariel's mom. I think it's nice what you're doing here. Ariel loves the field trips. She always has something to talk about! She learns a lot from them."

"Thank you!" he said, "I'm glad you allowed her to go on the trips. It's good to meet parents like you! Positive individuals."

I had to smirk at his comment, "Not too many around here."

"Are you new here?" he asked.

"I work evenings. You're used to seeing my sister. She woke up sick this morning and couldn't come in. Well, let me go get ready for the shift. It was nice meeting you."

"Same to you," he smiled.

Pastor Reynolds

❧

I stopped by the church after breakfast at the café. I checked in with Tameka before heading to my office. That was our routine.

"Hello Pastor!"

"Good morning sister. Any updates? Have you found a location for our next field trip for the youth?"

"I'm still working on that," she smiled.

"But I want you to know that I'm so proud of the project and its success over these few months. You have been a blessing to the children that participate."

That felt good to hear. "I'm only doing the work of God. He showed it to me and I did His will. Thank you for your help with it as well." She came around her desk and gave me hug—one I could tell she was trying to force.

It was time that I addressed her actions. I moved her body from mine.

"I'm sorry," she said.

I then knew we both were on the same page! We definitely needed to talk. I didn't want to discuss things in the church, it would be rather inappropriate. I invited her out to lunch on me. She accepted. I loved Italian and I learned she did too, so Italian it was.

"You're a very nice woman," I said to her after taking a sip of my iced tea, "You don't have to throw yourself at me."

She immediately stopped eating. She didn't know I had figured her out. She was very obvious. I saw that she was lost for words.

"I'll save us both the trouble. We're both individuals of God. You're walking in Christ. I'm one of his messengers. I don't see why we can't casually date."

She still was lost for words, but the smile she gave said that she was willing to casually date. I needed to clear up some things as well.

"I'm not one to rush things," I said.

"When I said casually date, I meant just that. We're both Christians. We will do things the right way (*the godly way*), and if things are meant to work out, God will see that they do."

Lauren

My hair salon was on the east side of town. My clientele was great! There were five stylists that worked for me, including myself. My business was doing extremely well. Kim sat in my chair as I rolled her hair. My stylists knew I did not like gossiping in the salon, but they did it anyway.

We over heard one say,

"Y'all new pastor has been seen out with Tamika!"

That definitely caught our attention. "What!!" I snapped.

Kim flipped through a magazine, "Girl, don't act shocked. I told y'all she was going to be after that man!"

The stylist gave us all the tea! The two had been out to eat around town, at each other houses and had even left the town on multiple occasions.

"She is up to no good" said Kim. "Pastor has to see that."

"He may not," I added.

She snapped, "Well, if he doesn't, he needs to go back and have a talk with God and make sure he received the right calling."

We couldn't help but to laugh at Kim! She just didn't care what she said or who was around.

"Y'all laughing, but I'm serious," she continued, "She's the devil in the flesh and if he keeps on fooling with her, I'mma be like Jesus and put them both out of Temple of Heaven!"

A stylist reminded us of Tamika's relationship with our previous pastor. She definitely spent that poor man's money.

"No one in the town has been seeing him buy her things like the last one did."

"Once a gold digger, always a gold digger," snapped Kim.

I sighed, "Yeah she robbed that poor man blind."

"The he left!" said Kim. "I wouldn't have left! I would have put her out."

Kim was starting to work my nerves. "Everyone doesn't believe in putting people out!"

"Temple of Heaven should!" she demanded.

Allison stormed into the salon with her black sun dress and blonde curls trailing behind her. She removed her shades and flopped down in a nearby styling chair.

"I thought it was a terrible, horrible rumor," she yelled as she twirled around and around in the chair.

"I just saw it with my own blue eyes! Tamika and Pastor just drove by!"

Kim then laughed, "We know, we know! Calm down before you sweat, your mascara gone run, then your makeup, and you gone look like the wife on Adams Family in the face!"

"Oh, hush Kim," snapped Allison. "This is not good!"

Kim threw her hands into the air, "What can we do! You and Lauren so holy, holy, holy. Y'all not gone interfere. So just say y'all little favorite line and leave it be."

I looked at Allison and she looked me. We both then said,

"We're placing it in God's hands."

"There ya go" said Kim. "Amen."

Audrey

✿

Ariel came home and told me Pastor Reynolds and the church was having a youth blast for the children in the town. I didn't get out much, plus I was tired from work. My baby knew that, but she begged me to go. So, we went. It was held behind the city hall. That wasn't hard to figure out why, the sides wouldn't dare cross to the other. It was very nice, despite the rejection. There were tons of activities and games. Musical chairs, cake walk, sack rack, pick a duck, go fishing, face painting and much more. Ariel was more interested in running to Pastor Reynolds as he was grilling food than playing games!

He turned around and picked her up, "Slow down. Smoke is over here."

We both made direct eye contact. Kind of

awkward, so I just smiled.

"You just got here, huh?" he asked her.

"Yes, I had to wait for Mommy to get off work."

"Well, it's plenty of games out here for you to play! Go have fun!"

"Thank you! Thank you!" she said as he placed her down.

She then began to pull me, "Come on Mommy."

"Hold on sweetie!" I laughed. My sister then took her hand and walked her over to the games.

"Ariel's teacher sent home a flyer about the pre-school graduation you are providing here at town-hall. That is nice of you and the church. I just wanted to say that."

"God placed it on my heart," he smiled.

"You're a great person and brave," I said. "You're the first pastor that has done things like this to bring both sides together."

Lauren

W e were painting faces at the youth
blast when Kim saw that Tameka was
headed our way.

"Look who's coming to join us," she
laughed.

Allison sighed, "Ugh! Why!" Kim was
so tickled, "We are close to the grill."
We looked toward the grill and saw a woman
standing with the pastor.

"Oooooh okay," I laughed.

"She's only coming over to get a closer
look," snapped Kim. "I'm not about to play
with her. We're not in church either! I'll tell
her a thing or two! She doesn't even like us!"

"Hey ladies," said Tameka moving closer to
the table.

"Hello Sister Johnson," said Allison.

"It was a nice a turn out," she said looking over at the grill. "That's exactly who I thought it was."

Kim snapped, "Oh please, you knew who it was way back there! She doesn't want your man! Her daughter is in the program!"

"I know which little girl is hers and the pastor is not my man!" snapped Tameka.

Kim laughed, "Well whatever y'all have going on, relax! God got ya back!"

Tameka smirked, "I have nothing to worry about."

Kim just continued to pick at her,

"So, you and pastor are not official."

Tameka ignored her of course, "I'm just worried about him being around her."

I had enough! Kim was my friend and I tolerated her, but I was not about to tolerate Tameka continuing to disrespect the young lady.

"You know nothing about her!" I snapped.

"Oh, I know," smirked Tameka.

"I would think that you would, but it's sad that you don't know the truth!" I said standing up from the table.

Her attitude was only making me angry.

"What's sad is that you believe her," laughed Tameka.

That comment right there made my blood boil. Tameka only knew gossip! That woman had not done anything to anyone in the town. Rich individuals allowed money to control their thoughts and look down on others. If she only took a look in the mirror. She would realize she was just the same. I couldn't do anything but walk away from the table. I was beyond upset. I knew my friends and Tameka knew it.

Pastor Reynolds

✤

As the young lady and I talked near the grill, I noticed that people were staring. Those that were sitting turned completely around. I was confused. There was a great deal of negative energy. I tried to ignore it.

"Your daughter is very smart and helpful to the other children. You're doing a great job with her."

I could tell she noticed the individual stares as she looked around. I saw she was uncomfortable. She then ended our conversation by saying,

"Well Pastor Reynolds, it was nice talking to you, but Ariel will be back over here to get my sister or me soon. She can be handful."

"Be blessed" I said.

"You too Pastor."

The youth blast was a success. I was tired! I wanted to go home and sleep. Tameka invited me over. I wanted to decline, but she wasn't going to like that. She and I were sitting on the couch in the living room area watching television.

"I think we should make the youth blast a yearly event," I suggested waiting for her opinion.

"I agree. You were real handsome at the grill."

I laughed at her. She was a character and I enjoyed spending time with her.

"Well, thank ya!"

"Oh no problem!" she laughed. "I'm a bit concerned about Ariel. I saw you talking to her mom at the grill."

Ariel was a sweet girl. I thought her mom was doing a great job with her. Every time she came on a field trip, she was in pretty good spirits. Her outside appearance didn't give off any concern. I was wondering exactly what Tameka was referring to.

"What about her?"

Tameka sighed "I'm concerned about her living environment. Her mother. She is not fit."

Tameka was not making any sense. I continued to think about the little girl. We asked teachers before every field trip who would need a lunch and Ariel was never on the list. She always had a lunch. Most kids would complain about things going on at home. She was not one of them.

The next day, I ended my day early at the church. I decided to stop by the café on the west side. I remembered Ariel's mother saying she worked in the evening. I drove onto the parking lot and saw her mother pacing outside of the café. She was on the phone and I could tell she was angry by her constant pacing and gestures. I walked up just as she was ending the call.

"Wrong time of day for you to be here," she laughed.

"I actually came to see you," I said.

She was indeed confused as I expected her to be. I told her it was about Ariel.

"Did something happen on a field trip?" she asked.

"No," I assured her. "A staff member of the program was concerned about you and Ariel.

If there is anything you need help with, please don't hesitate to call us. We want to make sure the living environment for Ariel is the best. She is a bright little girl….."

I could not finish my statement before the woman cut me off.

"What did you just say!" she snapped.

That was confirmation. I had made her upset. That was not my intention. She didn't spare me, she let me have all of it!

"You're new to this town! I really can't get mad at you! But I am mad at the people here! FYI Pastor, people around here talk and run their mouth! I don't know who ran their mouth to you at that church, but I take darn good care of my daughter. Excuse my tone! But you see my daughter! How dare you believe them and come to my job to sell me a pity plea. Bye Pastor!"

We were preparing to go on our next field trip to a museum not too far outside of town. Allison was responsible for taking roll. She informed me a student was missing. That student was Ariel. I went to the teacher's classroom and looked inside. Ariel was indeed sitting on the carpet playing with blocks. Her teacher informed me that her mother did not sign the permission slip for her to attend. Her mother was just that upset about the incident.

I knew she did not want to see me, but I headed back to the café after the field trip. I walked inside and saw the young lady dressed in a waitress uniform wiping the tables.

"We've stopped serving for the night," she said without looking up.

"You didn't allow Ariel to go on the field trip."

She stopped wiping the tables and looked up at me. She rolled her eyes, "She will not be in your program anymore."

"You can be upset about me coming here, but don't make her suffer," I pleaded.

The young lady tossed the towel on the counter, folded her arms and let me have it again.

"Look! This town is corrupted! I really sup-ported what you were doing! But you're just like everyone else! Listening to the bull crap and then believing it! Somebody had to tell you something for you to come to me with that! You would have come to me first! You didn't! You knew my daughter didn't appear to be living in an unfit environment to you! Therefore, you never said anything to me! Now if you would excuse me, I have about fifteen minutes of work left. Don't try to apologize!"

Well that didn't turn out too good. I was actually there to apologize. I felt bad. Everything she said was right. I had to apologize in some form. Ariel also needed to be back in the program. She enjoyed it.

"At least let me take you home?"

"I have legs!" she snapped.

"You wouldn't let me apologize...."

"Yeah you definitely can't take me home."

She was too angry and stubborn for crying out loud! I wasn't going to give up. I pleaded and pleaded until she got sick of me. I really didn't like the new impression she had of me. I was not that person.

"I normally don't allow people to take me home," she said standing outside of my car. "Since you're a pastor, I'm praying it's safe. You better not be one of those crooked pastors or one that will turn out to be a lunatic!"

I laughed, shook my head and opened the car door for her, "It's safe. You can trust me."

"No, I can't," she said getting into the car.

I closed the door for her and got in on the driver's side." Why is that?"

She smirked, "You live in Crestview."

I laughed, "But I'm not from here."

"Doesn't count!" she snapped, followed by smiling.

Maybe she was warming up to me again.

"Not for anything?"

"Nope!" she laughed.

"I never caught your name….." I said to her.

"You're asking for too much information."

She burst into laughter and so did I. She liked to joke around.

"I'm kidding, my name is Audrey."

I smiled, "Pretty name. Nice to meet you Audrey, I'm Daniel."

She directed me to her apartment complex. The dark red brick, two story building was not attractive at all, but who was I to judge? People were lingering outside random doors while clothes hung out other windows. Some windows were even taped or covered with garbage bags.

"Welcome to the west side," she said snapping her fingers at me and interrupting me while staring at the building. "Yeah, its everything you expected it to be, huh?"

"Can I walk you to your apartment?" I asked her.

She eyed me and said, "Yeah sure, and you can also come in to see what type of environment that is unfit for my daughter!"

"Can we let that go?" I begged.

"I'll think about it," she said opening the passenger door.

The inside of the apartment was not bad at all. I was greeted by a fragrance that I made out to be citrus rainforest. The living area was awfully clean with a grey and red theme. The kitchen area was spotless with a brown family table and four chairs. Ariel came running up to the living room. April was right behind her.

"You're supposed to be sleep!" snapped Audrey.

April ran back to the room. "Pastor! Audrey, you should have told me he was coming!"

We both laughed.

"I didn't know!" she yelled out.

She picked up her daughter, "I bet you were drawing and doodling huh. My little artist!"

"Yes, I was!" she smiled. "Pastor R, did you bring mama home?"

I was shocked at the comment made by the little one, but I answered yes. Her next remark made her mom and I both laugh,

"Mama did you tell Pastor R thank you?"

She hadn't told me thank you when I thought about it. "As a matter of fact, she didn't."

Ariel placed her hand over her mouth as if she was shocked, "Now Mama you know better."

She was the cutest little thing! We could not do anything but laugh at her. Audrey put her down, said good night to me and headed to bed.

"Thank you," said Audrey while turning to me.

"You're welcome," I smiled.

"I apologize."

She smirked, "It's okay. You didn't know. We might not live in the east side, but the living environment is fit. Might not be what they are used to over there, but it's okay. I'm taking care of my daughter. I will always take care of her."

"I see that. Will she be attending the next field trip?"

Audrey smiled, "I knew that was coming. She will be."

Audrey

🌱

It was time for my baby to graduate pre-school. I was so happy for her! She learned a lot! From writing her name to counting. She loved to draw! She would make my day by bringing home pictures she drew. I just put them all on our refrigerator.

We walked hand in hand into the city hall. Pastor Reynolds was greeting all the parents and children. Before we could even get to the door, I thought this man took a double-take at me dressed in my fitted below the knee, classy, conservative, red, nylon dress with my matching pumps. My thoughts were correct as we continued to walk towards him. I watched as his eyes stared at my shoes, traveled up my body, admired my loose curls and then became glued to mine, but I looked away. I was trying to pull his pastor card as a way of dismissing that he was admiring me. My baby saved him!

"Hey Pastor R!" she said, tapping his leg.

"Oh, hey Ariel!" he smiled. "I didn't see you there!"

I wanted to say, Yeah because you were too busy staring at her mama from north, south, east to west. Instead, I played like I was looking for something in my purse.

"Hey Audrey," he said to me.

"Hey Pastor," I smiled looking up from my purse, but avoiding eye contact with him.

The guest speaker was a local police officer. I thought it was neat how he spoke to the small children about making good and bad choices as they get older. I couldn't completely concentrate. I felt someone staring at me. It was definitely the pastor. He and I made eye contact and I quickly looked away. I couldn't keep trying to save this man by saying he was a pastor and he couldn't be looking at me. The only conclusion was that I was delusional, flat-out loosing my mind. Then I saw Tameka staring at me! That was the last person I wanted staring at me.

What was she looking at?

Why was she looking at me?

The west side Audrey wanted to stand up and ask her, but my east side mentality said not to.

I planned a small celebration for my baby and her accomplishment with two other parents from the apartment complex. We set up a small cake and punch at the park while our kids played. It wasn't much, but it was all we had. We sat at a bench while our kids played.

"What was that at town hall this morning?" asked my sister.

I had an idea of what she was referring to, but I played clueless. "What?"

I took a sip of punch and spit it right back out when she said,

"You and Pastor Reynolds in the doorway eye-sexing while the speaker was up talking!"

"I was not doing anything! He was not either! He has a woman, Tameka. At least that is the word around town."

My sister had noticed!

That was all the confirmation needed that I was not delusional. I could not pull his pastor card. The pastor was a human being after all, but I still was not about to accept that he was staring at me!

Not me, I'm from the west side, I couldn't dare be his type of woman.

Pastor Reynolds

❧

The field trips were successful, the youth blast was spectacular, and the graduation was phenomenal. It was time to find more ideas of outreach. I wanted to actually visit the west side and pass out pamphlets of programs we offered at the church. Just as they were with the other projects, some members were for it while others shot it down! We created an outreach committee and hit the streets.

I was assigned 36th Street. Members of the church called it prostitute avenue.

They did not want to go there. I took the dirty work. It needed to be done. I passed out pamphlets and some were accepting while others tried to bribe me. At the end of the street, I found myself standing in front of a strip club.

It read, "Live dancers, Men entertainment."

The front door opened, and a woman came out dressed in a long back black jacket in a pair of six-inch black stilettoes.

"Audrey…."

She quickly looked at me and stopped in her stride. I could see her heart pounding. It was about to jump out of her chest. She rushed away and I followed behind her, but she would not stop. She flagged down the nearest bus and quickly got on.

After services the following Sunday, Tameka wanted to go out to eat. I was not up to it. I had other things on my mind. I took her home. I told her I would call her later. I stood outside of Audrey's apartment. I took a deep breath before knocking. I knew she probably didn't want to see me after our last encounter.

I was relieved when I heard a little voice say, "Who is it?"

Thank God for the baby. "Pastor R," I said.

Ariel opened the door the for me. I picked her up, walked in and closed the door, "Is your Mama home?"

"Yes," said Ariel. "She's sleeping. I'll go get her."

Audrey

Why was this child shaking me? I had to be dreaming! I heard her say Pastor R was there in the apartment. Yep, I was dreaming. She kept on shaking me. I sat up in the bed and frowned at her. I then heard her say it again, "Mama! Pastor R is here!"

I was not dreaming!

What was he doing here!

I had to put some clothes on! That child let that man in my house and I only had on shorts and a sports bra! I pulled the covers back, rushed over to my dresser and pulled out the first shirt I saw! I slid in a pair of house shoes. Put my wild hair in a ponytail and walked out of the room. He was indeed standing in my living room.

"Hi Pastor. Ariel, I've told you about opening the door."

Ariel then said to me, "You said never to open the door for strangers. It's Pastor R! He's not a stranger Mama…"

That child was so smart that I wanted to smack myself sometimes for having her. I told him to have a seat and I would be out in a minute. I went inside the bathroom, but I did not close the door shut. I could hear the little smart child still talking.

"Mama is brushing her teeth. I know. Her breath has a funny smell when she wakes up."

Then that ole bucket head pastor had the nerve to laugh and the little seed of mine kept going. "She's brushing her teeth, so you won't smell it."

I walked up on them from the bathroom, "I heard you little grown girl! Go to your room please, just for a while."

I sat on the other couch away from him and waited for him to begin. I knew he was about to judge me like everyone else. I folded my arms, cocked my head to the side, crossed my legs, and prepared for the "how ungodly my actions were" speech.

"I didn't know you were sleeping, he said. I thought you were possibly getting ready for your shift at the café. I wanted to catch you before you left."

"I don't work on Sundays," I snapped. "Don't ask either, I'm not coming to that church."

"I'm not here for that. But I am curious; why not my church?"

"Church folks are messy. Especially the members of Temple of Heaven. Trust me. I know. You haven't been here long enough to know your members, but you will soon find out. I know why you're here. I don't feel like explaining it."

He smiled and said to me, "You don't have to explain anything to me. I just want to know why you ran off?"

"You were going to judge me! You're really here to preach to me! I'm ready."

He laughed and said, "I'm not here to judge you. I didn't judge you the other night."

"Well, that's why I left. You're a pastor and that's all they do around here!"

Pastor Reynolds made direct eye contact at me, "Listen, I don't know what other Pastors do around here. I can only speak for myself. It's not my place to judge anyone. God has that responsibility. I preach the word He gives and shows me to individuals, not judge them. You didn't have to leave. I want you to understand that I'm human just like you."

He reached into his back pocket and pulled out his wallet. He took a business card from it and handed it to me. I read his name, phone number, address, email, and the church name with service hours.

"I told you I wasn't coming!" I snapped.

"You said don't ask. I didn't say a word. I just handed you a business card."

"But you want me to come."

"I would like for you to come," he smiled.

Pastor Reynolds

My next idea for outreach was to read Bible stories to the children who visited the community library. The coordinator was on board and we scheduled to meet there to discuss the plans. I walked into the library and saw Audrey upstairs on a computer. I was headed her way when she saw me. She laughed and shook her head.

"What's funny, Miss Audrey?" I asked in full voice.

"Um this a library," she whispered. "I'm going to need you to lower your voice."

"What's funny, Miss Audrey?" I whispered.

"You're funny! You look funny," she laughed.

I laughed and glanced at her screen. It read "University of Balmore". She was completing an assignment.

"You're in school. This is why you dance as a second job. To pay for school."

She lowered her head, "Yeah tuition has to be paid. While Ariel is with my sister at the café, I'm here. I work at the café in the evening, I dance at night."

"I teach online classes," I smiled.

"You do not!" she said. "Wait. That means you're old!"

I laughed. I knew I was older than her. Any person could see that.

"What, you're about 24?" I asked her.

"Correct, and you're about 44!"

"Not that old young buck!"

"Well 54, you old geezer."

"Harsh!"

"Well, you called me a young buck! So, I bucked back," laughed Audrey. "How old are you seriously?"

"I am 34 years old."

"Still old!" she laughed.

"Keep laughing. I have yet to see you at church."

She responded by saying, "You have yet to get new members."

I laughed and then I replied, "I understand some members in churches are messy. But don't let their behavior deter you from God. They need some work, I know. That's why God sent me.

"Shoot, they need a whole lot of work, Pastor!"

"Remember, Jesus didn't come to heal the well, but he came to heal the sick. In time, God is going to use me to help elevate them."

Winking at her, I said, "They may be just where they need to be."

Smiling back, she replies, "Hmmm."

Audrey

Bills were getting higher and higher. I really needed help from Ariel's dad. My bills were so high that my baby was starting to suffer, and she didn't deserve that. I was doing all I could. The help of my sister was beginning to not be enough. I had to call Corey. I hated calling him, but if I didn't call him, he wasn't trying to call me to see what she needed either. He showed up to the café. I met him outside and he handed me twenty dollars. He knew that was not going to help me!

"What is this!" I yelled. "You bring me less money every time!"

"I have to live too!" he yelled back.

"Your daughter does too! I make sacrifices! You have a full-time, salary paid job and you show up with this!"

He moved closer to me and said, "I'm not giving you no more money, take that and be happy. You only gone use it on yourself anyway."

"That's your new wife in your ear— the one that you cheated on me with! Tell her I said every piece of nothing you give me goes on your daughter! Make sure you also tell her that I'm putting you on child support since she wants to keep running her mouth! Less money in her house!"

"Do what you got to do," he snapped in my face before walking to his car and speeding away.

Next to his car was Pastor Reynold's car. He got out and looked at me. I knew he heard everything. I couldn't control the tears if I tried, but him being there and hearing that only made more fall.

He then said to me, "Whatever is going on, pray about it and let God have it."

Pastor Reynolds

I didn't want anymore food after hearing that man talk to Audrey like that. His actions added more confirmation that she was just a single mother trying to care for her child the best way she could. The entire situation made me angry. I also thought about Tameka and her involvement with the rumors. I headed to her house. There was no need to knock; I used the key she had given me. She was typing on her computer in her office.

"Sweetheart, we need to talk," I said.

She turned around in her computer chair, "Hey, I didn't know you were coming over. What do we need to talk about?"

"Ariel, the little girl in the program."

"Yeah I remember, with the unfit mother."

I didn't waste any time getting to the point, "Glad you said that. That's why we need to talk. I've been to her home. Her living environment is fit. Therefore, I need to ask you something. Have you been listening to gossip or gossiping? I hope not. I don't like it. I don't condone it. You like to talk about marriage. I will not have my first lady involved in nonsense. It's not lady-like. If we ever get to the planning stages of that, this gossip will have to stop!"

"This happens all too often at churches: all the gossip and rumor-spreading. And Tameka, I won't allow it. One reason gossip is a sin is because it sows discord among others. It's a reason so many of us are divided, even in the church. God is not pleased with it. I won't allow it in my relationship. I won't condone it in my church."

I had nothing more to say to her. She had been involved in mess. God led me to Audrey's situation outside of the café for me to fully understand on my own. The woman that I was casually dating was clearly involved in gossip that was hurting the lives of others.

Audrey

❧

My baby and I had been grocery shopping. We were singing the ABC song. When we walked into the apartment, I flipped the light switch, but the light did not come on. I rushed into the kitchen and flipped that light switch, it didn't come on. The lights had been turned off. I threw the groceries and my purse to the floor. I tried so hard to keep my lights from being cut off. I failed. My baby seeing the lights off hurt the most. I fell to the floor in tears.

I felt her little hands rub my back,

"It's going to be okay Mama. Pastor R said when we are in trouble or sad we should pray. He said to pray means to talk to God."

She was absolutely right.

Was God using my baby to speak to me?

Was he using Pastor Reynolds to speak to

me?

I remembered the day outside of the café when he told me to pray.

"Pastor R was right baby," I said to her. "Come on, let's pray together."

I hadn't prayed to God in a long time. That day I did go to him. Not only did I go to him, but I went to him with my baby girl by my side.

I dropped Ariel off at the café with my sister. I needed to get to the library! I had a final exam in a class. The bus dropped me off in front of the library. I went to the door, but it was locked. A sign read the library was closed for the day. I panicked! I could not afford to fail the class! What was I going to do! I didn't have a computer at home! Who had a computer on the west side? Nobody! I began to pace to gather my thoughts. That wasn't working. I stopped and right where I stood, I began to pray.

Pastor Reynolds

❧

I was driving in my car on my way home. As I passed the library, I thought I saw a woman kneeled down. What was she doing? Then I realized it was Audrey. I drove onto the library parking lot, got out of my car and walked a little closer. She was praying.

"Amen," she said.

"Praying outside of the library...." I said.

She immediately rushed over to me, "You teach online classes! You have a computer at home! That means you have Wi-Fi! Which means I can take my final! I won't fail my test! I can take it at your house? Thank God!"

I wanted to burst into laughter, but I could tell even though she was losing her mind and although it was funny to me, she was serious. We headed back to my house and I allowed her to use my office computer to take her test. She saw the many high school sports pictures of me on the wall.

"You played football," she smiled. "Look at you!"

"All around sportsman!" I bragged, "Well here's my computer. I'm going to get comfortable and I'll be back to check on you? Do you want anything to drink? A snack?"

She told me should like water. Before getting her water, I changed into black basketball shorts and a muscle shirt. That was my outfit of comfort. I had to add my socks and flip flops. I took a glass of water into the office and sat it on the desk.

"What's your major?"

"I'll talk to you after I finish this exam! And you're the college professor!" she laughed.

I took the hint and left my office. I went to relax on my couch and watch a little TV. I was flipping through channels after an episode of Law and Order when she walked into the living room.

"Did you pass?"

She began to dance, "A 95%."

I laughed, "That's great 'Miss Get Out', so I can take my test. Put me out of my own office."

"I did not say that," she laughed.

"Yeah you did," I laughed. "Sit down, rest yourself. I prepare college exams. I know they can be tough and besides you're done, you can talk to me now."

Audrey eyed me and then flopped down on my loveseat away from me. She didn't trust me and that was fine. I was not going to harp on it.

"What's your major?"

"Animal Science."

"Noooo way! So little ticking time bomb won't explode for a puppy!"

"Shut up!" she laughed, "But yes I love animals."

"Oh, you want to be a vet, huh?"

"I will own an animal hospital!" she snapped. "Just got to get to veterinarian school. I want to give Ariel the best!"

"What about you?"

"I want the best too, but my child is more important than anything I want."

I had to encourage her by telling her she

was a wonderful mother,

"If all mothers were like you, a lot of the kids I see in the program would have a better life."

She then said, "If all mothers were like me, they wouldn't survive. Not all women know how to do that the correct way. Yeah, dance, but the people around here judging me wouldn't know how to survive if they were in my shoes. I have a responsibility. My daughter. I know working in the café and dancing is not going to give her the life she deserves. That's why I'm going to school, but I have to pay for school. The café pay check couldn't do both and to be honest, both of them together are still a struggle."

I told her to keep praying, "Ariel told me on the field trip that you two prayed together because the lights are off at home."

Audrey lowered her head and sighed. She leaned back and covered her face, "They are."

I wanted to be a blessing to her, but I knew she would deny it, "Let me help you." She got up from the couch. I could tell she was uneasy by that question.

"I'll be fine," she said shuffling with her

clothes. "I can't. Um can you please take me home? Thanks for allowing to use your computer."

Audrey

My baby girl and I had so much fun at the park. She loved to play hide and seek or for me to push her high on the swings. We made it home and she wanted me to light a candle so that she could draw. Just as I opened the cabinet to get a candle, the lights came on. My sister then ran into the living room screaming my name. I rushed out of the kitchen to see what the fuss was about.

"The café. It burned!"

"What!" I yelled. "No! We have bills! The lights just came back on! Now we can't keep them on!"

My sister then said, "The pastor from Glory Rose on this side was there to help. He will have a food bank for employees at the church every Monday night starting this Monday."

That was some relief, but not enough. I walked over to my couch and sat down. I covered my face. All I could do was scream.

"If it's not one thing, it's another!"

April then said, "Since you said that I may as well keep the other thing to myself."

I then wondered what my sister had to tell me. I somewhat knew. I was once 19 years old pregnant with Ariel. She didn't have to tell me. I knew why she was sick all those mornings and couldn't go to work. She started to cry and all I could do was wrap my arms around her and assure that everything would be okay. She wasn't convinced.

"How do we know everything is going to be okay."

I sighed and said, "We're going to pray and allow God to take control over everything."

I took my sister's hand, she took Ariel's hand, and we made a small circle. I prayed to God and asked him to take each and every burden into his hand that my family was carrying. I encouraged my sister and daughter to not worry because God would take care of us.

Glory Rose on the west side did just as they said they would. There was a food bank for the employees. We stood in line and waited to be served. We noticed other churches were there volunteering. I saw Pastor Reynolds carrying a box for a family outside. When coming back in, we made eye contact. I smiled and that signaled for him to come on over. As always, my baby almost did a back flip!

"Pastor R!!"

"Hey there Ariel," he said. Followed by picking her up, as always! He put her down and took the box from my hand, "Let's go ladies!"

"So, you're taking us home?" I asked staring at him.

He mocked me and said, "So, you're gone ride the bus with this big box?"

Ariel then had to go the bathroom. My sister took her while he and I headed to his car.

"Thank you," I said. "For taking us home and paying my light bill."

He smiled at me, "No problem."

"How did you do it? You don't have any of my information!"

Pastor Reynolds stopped and said, "When God gives you a task, you might know how

He wants you to do it, but he will guide you. By the way, I also took care of your bills and rent for six months."

I couldn't believe what he had just said! That was so generous of him. He put the box down on the ground to open his truck and I just hugged him!

Pastor Reynolds

I stopped by Tameka's house. The plan was to have dinner, but she hadn't been acting herself lately. That was strange. It was very weird. When I got to her house, she was cooking in the kitchen. She knew I was there, but she ignored me. She didn't speak or anything. I knew something was bothering her.

I decided to go ahead and talk. I knew she would not.

"Would you like to talk about it?"

She still didn't talk to me. She just kept cooking like I was not even there. She knew how to upset me, but I was trying to not get there.

"We planned to have dinner tonight and enjoy the evening, but I feel like this is not going to be enjoyable," I said sitting down at the bar.

She blatantly asked, "Are you seeing Audrey?"

I had to admit, Audrey was an attractive woman and Tameka was not changing her ways—becoming more and more unattractive to me as the days grew, but I was not seeing Audrey.

"You know the answer to that!" I snapped.

Tameka then yelled, "You have been seen coming out and going in to her apartment. She was at your house. You paid her bills. So, no I don't know the answer to that!"

"That is all true!" I yelled back, "So I can't help the people of this community?" I then knew she had been listening to gossip.

"Same ole Tameka! Listening to foolishness!"

She threw the spoon she was stirring the mashed potatoes with into the sink, "Everyone is talking about it! I was bound to hear it!"

"But you don't have to believe it!" I yelled standing up from the bar! She and I stood face to face, arguing. She was heated, and I was off the Fahrenheit scale.

"Just because I am helping her does not mean I'm seeing her! The first time I went over there was to see about Ariel. I told you that! The second time was because I didn't want her to see me as a horrible person just like the rest of the people in this town! She was at my house taking an exam for a class because the library was closed."

"Why does it matter how she views you if you are not seeing her!" yelled Tameka.

Out of everything I said, that is all she heard. That didn't help my anger at all.

I just kept yelling and yelling until I was turning red!

"I am a true man of God! Clearly this town has not had one in a long time. I was passing out flyers and I ran into her…"

"Coming out of the strip club! This whole town knows about the strip club!"

I was done. I didn't want to hear any more about the town and their gossiping habits.

"I don't care Tameka! I'm here to do the will of God!"

"Well, whatever!" she said. "I saw you with my very own eyes hugged up outside of Glory Rose."

I couldn't do anything but laugh. I was so angry with her. I didn't want to say anything I would regret or didn't mean so I just said,

"The devil has been working on you I see. Audrey was so thankful and grateful for what I did for her that she showed her appreciation with a hug. When you begin to rebuke the devil, let me know."

Audrey

I sat on a swing in the park and just thought about my life. My baby sister was standing in the shoes I stood in five years ago. My daughter thought I was the best mama in the world, but I knew she deserved better and I was just living life day by day.

A familiar car entered the park and I just stared at it. I really didn't feel like dealing with Pastor Reynolds, but that was his car. He sat on the swing next to me, "Hey…."

"Hi," I said shoveling my feet in the rocks as if I was a little lost girl.

"I stopped by your apartment to check on you all. Your sister looked like she had just woken up."

I couldn't help but to laugh. I knew exactly how April looked when she first woke up!

"She told me you probably went for a walk. I thought I would come find you. I need to go for a walk myself."

"Everything good?" I asked him.

"Could be better, but prayer fixes all," I assured her.

"Yeah you're right but seems to me like you want to talk about it."

He got up and leaned against the swing, "I'm quite sure you already know. I know you know."

I knew what he was talking about and I didn't want to say I told him so, but I said, it. "I told you so".

He then expressed his feelings to me, "It amazes me how people can turn positive actions into negative ones. It's like they don't think."

I got up from the swing and began to walk. He followed of course, "That's the residents of Crestview."

He explained he knew it would be a bit challenging because the town was small, but he hadn't been here that long for so much to happen. I had to let him know he was handling the pressure well. The fact that he was making a difference was the main reason why the people were constantly gossiping. He needed to be reminded that the people were not used to positivity. He needed to know that he was not the only pastor being talked about. Before he came, the town always talked about the pastor of Glory Rose. He also needed to be reminded that he was the first to try to bring both sides together. He must have forgotten that people don't like change. I could tell he was listening and taking it all in, but him being Pastor Reynolds, he was always concerned about others.

"How have you been handling it?" he asked me.

I had to let him know I had more important things to worry about other than the people gossiping in town. I had been dealing with them way before he came into town. Them talking more now that he was helping me almost didn't phase me. He had been a blessing to my family. I knew that, he knew that, and God knew. I was not focused on the negativity. I was used to Crestview and their shenanigans. Mainly because they judged us (the women) that worked at the club. But they didn't know the whole truth. Even if they did, they would still make up lies. Especially about me. Every woman did not strip, myself included. I danced only. Table top and inter-missions between the strippers. No clothes ever left my body, but regardless people talk-ed.

" Glad you explained" he said to me.

"You thought I stripped huh?" I said shak-ing my head.

"I really didn't know, but now I do."

"Well next time you hear someone say I strip, do me a favor, don't defend me."

"What? Why not?"

There was no need. I had been dealing with the rumors since I was 17 years old. It was nothing new. I had been working there. I was on my own. My mother was not there. I couldn't remember the last time I had a mother. I knew he was going to ask questions, so I just stopped him before he did and told him I was not going to talk about my child-hood. I decided to show him where I go to clear my mind. Maybe it would help him. I took him to a large field of sun flowers! I loved when they blossomed in the summer.

"This is beautiful," he said to me.

I noticed him watching me. I think he was trying to read me.

"Something else is bothering you," he said to me.

He was right, but I really was not up for talking about it. I kept quiet and picked a sunflower. I inhaled the flower. He gently pulled it from me,

"You know you can talk to me about anything."

I was learning that about him. He was a very good listener and he was not judgmental. He was becoming a great friend of mine.

We saw the sun was starting to set. It was his idea to head back. I agreed. He offered to take me home and I accepted. He drove me home and began to talk about a summer program for the youth he and church members were putting together. He wanted Ariel to attend and I told him she would be there.

"We will need chaperones and staff. It will be a paid job."

I knew he was trying to ask me to work the summer camp. I did need the job. The café was in the process of being rebuilt and the income would help me care for Ariel. I told him I would think about it.

"I'll bring you an application," he said parking in front of my apartments.

Lauren

Pastor asked me to assist with the summer program since I did well with the field trips. I enjoyed working with the youth. I had no issue with helping. I would need some help of course. He gave me permission to pick staff to join me. I had to ask Kim and Allison. They agreed to help, but it's not like they had a choice! We always did things together.

We sat in his office at the church reviewing the applications of individuals that applied to work. Tameka peeped her head into the office,

"Hey ladies, are you all going through the applications for the summer program?"

She knew we were going through the applications, I don't even know why she asked. Kim checked her before I did, "You're not on this committee, we would appreciate it if you would leave."

"I need to review the applications!" snapped Tameka, "I will be doing the interviewing."

She was lying, and I knew it.

"Pastor said he would be doing the interviewing"

Tameka picked up the applications from the table any way. We all knew why she was looking through them. The town was talking. Pastor had been seen out more with Audrey than with Tameka.

"Her application is not in there!" snapped Kim. "Bye!"

Pastor then walked into the office, "Sister Lauren, you didn't tell me about sister Tameka being on the committee."

"She's not." I said.

"Well in that case, is there anything I can help you with sister Tameka?" he asked.

"No there is not!" she snapped. She dropped the applications on the desk and walked out of the office.

"Ladies when you're done, let me know of the selections," he said smiling at us. When we heard the office door close, we burst into laughter.

"Wow!" laughed Kim, "I almost laughed in her face!"

"Glad you didn't," I said. "I would have not been any good!"

"All that tension!" laughed Allison.

"Yes, I felt it," I said.

"Well you know what that means," said Kim. "He called her Sister Johnson! They aren't together."

It was the first day of the summer camp. Workers were arriving. I was assigning them tasks and handing out schedules. Kim and Allison were my assistants. Tameka was there to help with the older group of children. Audrey walked into the room and over to me. Her application was not in the stack. We did not select her, but I was not about to question her. Somebody sent her and I knew exactly who did!

"Hey Lauren," she smiled.

"It's good to see you Audrey."
"I was told that I could work with the younger group of youth."

I smiled, "You sure can."

We were eating lunch in the fellowship hall of the church. Tameka walked over to us, "Audrey's application was not in the stack!"

"You big mad huh," laughed Kim.

"Don't start with me!" snapped Tameka. "Who hired her?"

"I think you feel threatened by her. The entire town is talking, she showed up to work without the committee selecting her, and you're worried," snapped Kim.

"Never threatened by her! So, which one of you did it to piss me off!"

Kim laughed and laughed, "Your man, her man, I don't know who he belongs to, but Pastor had to. We didn't see her application!"

Tameka clearly was upset. She rolled her eyes and Kim and walked away.

"That was harsh," laughed Allison.

"She's a big girl, she'll be alright," shrugged Kim.

Pastor Reynolds

❧

The first day of camp was great! We were cleaning, preparing to go home for the day. I was mopping the floor when I heard singing. It was coming from Audrey's room. I stuck my head in and she was singing His Eye Is on the Sparrow as she wiped the tables. Her voice was so angelic that I could only listen. I was not going to dare interrupt her. When she finished, I stepped into the room.

"Beautiful voice."

She smiled at me, "Thank you!"

"How was your first day?"

"It was good. Thank you again for the job."

Ariel then ran into the room, "Be careful out there. It's wet," I said. "How did you like camp?"

"I had fun! My teacher let me draw! Are

you taking us home? You should stay and eat. Mama is cooking spaghetti and meatballs. My favorite!"

Audrey's mouth dropped completely to the floor, "Hold up now! You just can't invite people to our house."

"Mama, he is not people; he is Pastor R."

I loved the kid! She was so smart and funny! There was nothing Audrey could say to her. Instead, she covered her face and laughed.

"Um! I am hungry and I'm not doing anything later," I said.

Audrey took her hand down, "Really, you're going to feed into her."

I picked up Ariel, "Looks like I'm eating some of Mama's spaghetti! Thank you so much."

Ariel laughed, "You're welcome."

I knocked three times and Audrey opened her front door. I tried to control myself, but I couldn't stop my eyes from wandering. She always wore these fitted flirtatious, yet sophisticated type dresses that captured my undivided attention. The old me would have licked my lips, but the pastor in me said, "Get behind thee devil!" She was beautiful despite every thought that may have crossed my mind.

"You look nice."

Ariel then ran to the door, "She wore the dress for you. You got nice for her too! I like your tie!"

Audrey blushed by turning away, "Ariel stop it!"

Dinner was amazing. She could cook very well. I enjoyed it. She made sure Ariel was tucked into bed before joining me again in the living. She sat next to me on her couch. That was new. She always sat away from me. I didn't want to eat and run, I mentioned a movie and waited for her to make an excuse or flat-out tell me no. She didn't do either one. I was shocked! She was fine with watching a movie with me.

She went back to her room and came back with a stack of movies in her hand,

"Um, you're a pastor, but my movies aren't so pastoral-like. So here are all of Ariel's."

She smiled big and flopped down on the couch. She was hilarious. I took the movies and began to look through them. I chose Finding Nemo and she burst into laughter,

"Not at all! Ariel walks around saying the just keep swimming line like she's Dory."

My next choice was Happy Feet. I had actually watched it before. She agreed on that movie.

I felt someone shaking my shoulders. I opened my eyes to April shaking Audrey. Audrey opened her eyes and squinted them at April.

"Rise and shine!" laughed April.

Audrey sat up from my arms and said, "Stop playing with me April."

April kept laughing, "I'm not playing! Rise and shine you two."

Audrey's eyes widened, "Tell me I'm dreaming!"

"Not at all," laughed April. "Good morning."

"It's okay," I said. "We just fell asleep."

Audrey got up and began to pace, "You spent the night at my house! Your car was out there all night! People already talk! They are really going to talk now!"

April sat down on the couch laughing, "Yall are already the talk of this town. It will be nothing new. Calm down sis! Yall were cute sleeping!"

"April!" snapped Audrey.

"Sorry, I forgot yall are just friends…" laughed April.

Audrey

❧

We sponsored a trip to a water park for the youth of the summer program not far from the town. I was inside the women's dressing room changing. I was not alone. Tameka came out of a stall. She approached me at the sink.

"So, how did you get hired?"

I was not about to play with her, but then again, I wanted to see her get worked up. I knew she had been listening to the town. Tameka was one of those type of people, so I had a little fun.

"I completed an application and submitted it."

"You did not," she said.

"I was on the committee and none of the members saw your application."

She knew that I knew Daniel was the director of the program. She knew he hired me.

"I can't help what you saw, but I know what I did."

Tameka tried to get under my skin by saying, "I know what you did too. You do it for a living."

I really didn't have time for her. I was enjoying picking with her, but I just wanted her to say what she had to say.

"Just get it all off your chest," I smirked.

Tameka stepped closer to me, "Stay away from Daniel."

That was it! I knew it! I decided to keep picking with her. She shouldn't have stepped to me.

"There it is! You feel better?"

"You heard me!" snapped Tameka.

Pastor Reynolds

🌿

Audrey walked out of the women's changing room. I was at a nearby water slide with a group of students. I took my shades from my swim trunks pocket and put them on my face to cover my eyes. They were about to wander all over her body. I didn't want anybody to see me.

The girl stayed making the color red look good. I remembered the red dress she wore to the graduation that had me forgetting I was greeting parents. Now, kids were about to drown because her body had all my attention in the red bikini.

I dropped Audrey and her family off after the swimming trip. I went home to shower. As I showered, I couldn't get her off of my mind. It was so bad that I headed back over to her place.

She opened her front door. Her hair was wrapped in a towel. She wore a robe.

"Daniel! Um, I was showering. Excuse my robe. Come on in. You should have called. What's up?"

I needed to know if Ariel or April was there. She told me they were sleeping.

"Okay, that means I need to be quiet," I said.

"What are you talking about?"

I was done holding back. She was very attractive. I was more than physically attracted to her. I was mentally and emotionally attracted to her. I was done being her friend, but I didn't know how to tell her. I showed her instead. I pulled her to me and kissed her. She pulled away and slowly opened her eyes. She was shocked. I was hoping I didn't scare her or make her uncomfortable. I decided to apologize.

"My bad, I just didn't know how to..."

"Don't apologize," she said walking back over to me and kissing me. I couldn't help but to indulge. As I wrapped my arms around her, she pulled away a second time. This time she went over to the couch and sat down. I did the same. We were speechless. But we needed to talk. She agreed that we needed to get things cleared up.

"Tameka! Are yall together?" She asked me.

I was not about to lie to her. Tameka and I were only casually dating technically, but that turned into more. Something that I had not ended properly, but it was one that I was going to end the correct way. She told me Tameka told her to stay away from me, but that wasn't her place. Tameka and I were not together.

"Well, I'm telling you what she told me. I have enough going on in my life. I don't need extra drama if I go there with you."

I tried to make her understand there would not be any drama. She was not believing me. She felt it was already drama with the gossiping around the town about us. I thought she was ignoring them. She always said she had been dealing with it before I came along. What was the issue now?

"Is there something else going on?" I asked without hesitation.

She didn't reply. She lowered her head. Her actions spoke for her. I needed her to talk to me. She would not. She just kept saying that she couldn't.

"Listen," I said to her. "We can start slow. I won't rush you. We can even continue to be friends. I want to be more, but I'll cherish our friendship."

I wanted to make her smile. I knew exactly what to say that would get her to laughing,

"You were looking mighty good in that bikini."

She burst into laughter and fell into my arms covering her face.

"Was I?" she teased.

I had to play along with her; I liked to see her smile, "Yes ma'am!"

"You seem to lose all control when I wear the color red," she teased some more. "Is that your favorite color?"

Red was indeed my favorite color. I couldn't help but stare at her. Temptation clearly was knocking on my doorstep. I asked her to excuse me because I couldn't resist.

I leaned in to kiss her and she moved back,

"You're a pastor! What do you mean you

can't resist! You better get it together!"

"I'm a man too!" I said.

Audrey eyed me and slid away from me. I then knew I needed to clear up what I was saying, "Wait, let me explain. When I said I can't resist, I was not referring to the sin of fornication. I was referring to kissing you. I'm extremely attracted to you and I've been wanting to kiss you for the longest. I just did, and it was everything I imagined, but let me make it clear: I will not have sex outside of marriage.

Audrey

✿

I was straightening my classroom like I did every day. Tameka walked in. She was pathetic in my opinion. I knew she was there to talk about Daniel. I was not shocked at all.

"What now?" I laughed.

"You clearly didn't hear me the first time when I told you to stay away from him," she said. "I saw yall leaving today."

"Well, you're clearly talking to the wrong person."

"It's you that I should be talking to."

"No! You should be talking to him. I'm not the one he's casually dating. Oh, I forgot, you two are no longer engaging in that," I laughed.

Tameka became real mad after I said that, "You don't know anything!"

"I do," I laughed, "Daniel and I are friends, friends tell each other things you know."

She started to walk towards the door, "This is my final time telling you to stay away from him!"

"I don't think I will," I said sitting down in my rolling chair.

Tameka quickly turned back toward me, "What you say?"

I smirked, "You heard me. I'm going to continue to cook him dinner. I'm going to accept every invitation he brings to me, and every time he allows his lips touch mine, oh, I will engage."

"You're such a hoe" snapped Tameka.

"So, should I be a gold digger?" I laughed.

"Don't forget I know about you," she said to me.

I acted in my flesh. I needed to stand my ground, but I could've handled it better.

I'm better than that, I thought.

Lord, I'm sorry I even allowed her to let me lose control a minute ago.

My flesh wanted me to continue picking with her, but that's just not my character.

So, instead of saying what my flesh really

wanted me to say, I simply said, "You think you know. You and I both know that I know all about you." Daniel then walked into the room. He immediately stopped at the sight of both of us. He told me to me to meet him at his car.

Pastor Reynolds

"Meet her at your car!" yelled Tameka to the top her of lungs.

I was not about to argue with her. Tameka would go on and on. I just had to tell her what was on my mind.

"You had no right to tell her to stay away from me. We are not together. I don't know what happened here, but leave her alone. You and I are done. You can address me if you have any questions."

I didn't take Audrey home that day.

We went to my house. Nothing special, we just wanted to spend time with one another. I wanted to show her something that was dear to me. One thing that I loved to do. I took her upstairs to a room that held a white piano.

"It is beautiful," she said walking over to it.

"Can you play?"

"Love to play," I smiled.

"Will you?"

"Only if you sing!"

She said that she would sing. I was excited to play while she sang. She couldn't figure out a song she wanted to sing. I just began to play. She then rushed away and out of the room. That was awkward. I stopped playing and followed her. I grabbed her just as she was about to go down the steps.

"What's going on?"

She didn't want to tell me. She began to fight me as usual when she did not want to talk about something.

"You can't keep things from me," I yelled in frustration.

"We're not together," she yelled back.

"But I care!"

I watched as tears began to fall down her face. I took her into my arms. I was done yelling. That was not helping the situation. She looked at me and asked, "Will you pray with me? I haven't prayed about a certain situation in a long time and I need to."

Audrey

❧

Daniel opened the emergency room door of the hospital for me. I rushed in and we made our way to the waiting room. I could not gather my thoughts, let alone control my tears. I saw my sister pacing.

"What happened?" I cried.

My sister had taken Ariel to a local food mart for ice cream. They were leaving the store when a car came driving past with guys shooting guns. She promised me she covered Ariel and pulled her back into the store. When they hit the floor, she realized my baby girl had been shot.

I screamed out in sadness and lost all my balance. Daniel helped me to my feet and sat me down in a nearby chair. He wiped my tears and tried to calm me down. I couldn't even focus on anything he was saying to me. I was worried about my daughter.

We were told by the doctors a bullet punctured her lung. The lung was beginning to close and surgery was required to stop the closing. She had been rushed to surgery to solve the issue because the lung was closing rapidly. My baby could lose her life. I left the waiting area and headed for the chapel. I kneeled at the front to pray and I noticed Daniel was kneeling with me.

I found myself at the field of sunflowers. My thoughts of my princess led me there. She had been in the hospital for a week. She had lost so much blood and things were not looking good for her.

Lauren

Y"ou still come here?" I asked her. Audrey slowly turned around at the sound of my voice. I knew she was not expecting to see me. Her eyes filled with tears, but none fell.

"This was our getaway as children during the summer," I said walking toward my childhood friend.

The trapped tears then poured down her face. I hugged my friend. I apologized for everything that happened between us.

She told me it wasn't my fault. I felt it was. I should've been there for her. I was not and that hurt for so many years. I was willing to rebuild our friendship. Audrey was willing as well. That made me feel better. I knew her daughter was not doing well, but Audrey was strong.

"I wish I would have been strong like you are back then," I said to her.

She said to me, "Then, what? You would have been living like I am too."

I cried out to her, "Audrey I don't want to live like this anymore."

Audrey shook her head at me, "Stop it please. I don't want to go back there."

"But you won't be alone this time," I assured her.

"Lauren, I can't."

"Audrey please," I pleaded.

"He walks around this town like..." She couldn't bear anymore. I could tell she was becoming angry.

"I know okay!" she yelled out.

Pastor Reynolds

Audrey reminded me a lot of my mother. I believe that is another reason why I was so attracted to her. She was very dedicated to the needs of her daughter. She went to the hospital every day to see her. Ariel wasn't responding. She had slipped into a coma and things were not improving. I walked into the hospital room and saw Audrey staring at her. She then rubbed her hand down her cheek, grabbed her hand and began to pray. As she prayed asking God to heal and strengthen Ariel, her little eyes opened.

Praise God! She tried to speak. The muffled sounds caught Audrey's attention. Audrey smiled and kissed Ariel on the forehead.

Ariel was able to discharge sooner than we

thought. That was nothing but God. Audrey packed her things while I read her a book. I finished the book and needed to talk to Audrey about something that was heavy on my spirit. She and I stepped out into the hallway,

"For your safety, come move into my house and I'll find a separate smaller apartment for myself," I said.

Audrey was not so sure about that. She was concerned that the new rumor would be we were shacking up. I wasn't concerned about that. I was worried about her and her family. Audrey wouldn't have been herself if she didn't fight me back on it.

"That's more bills on you. I can't afford your bills!" she said.

"I'm not asking you to pay the bills." I said.

"Well, I can't okay. I can take care of them! We will be fine."

I loved how independent she was. I just wanted her to put that aside so that I could help her. As much as she didn't want to, she took me up on my offer. She had to be difficult. Instead of living in my place, she allowed me to rent her an apartment on the east side of town. I didn't think it would stop the gossip or rumors.

Audrey

I did not want to move into Daniel's house. No way, no how! He wasn't going to give up, so I settled on him renting a two-bedroom apartment for my family. I did not like that it was on the east side, but I really didn't have a choice. Daniel and I were dating, so I had to consider his opinion. He cared about us and I knew that.

My day was not going well. I had been working on an assignment all day that was driving me crazy. I heard my front door open. It had to be April or Daniel, no one else had a key. The kiss on my cheek told me it was Daniel.

"What's going on?" he asked.

"This assignment is about to make me throw the whole computer out the window."

He turned me around the chair and pulled me up from the seat, "Sounds like you need a break."

"I really do with all the other things on mind," I said.

"Like what?" he asked me.

I really needed to talk to him, but I couldn't bring myself to say what I needed to say. Oftentimes, Daniel would scare me with his perfect responses. No man ever said the things he said to me. I never knew what was coming next after I said something to him. I just said what was on my mind.

"I quit the club."

He smiled at me. I knew he was happy. He never pressured me to quit. He didn't have to. What man wanted the woman they cared about dancing at a club?

"What made you quit?" he asked me.

That was the line that I was scared to respond to. He was going to come back with a perfect line.

"You." I said.

The perfect line was, "Well if you're ready, we can move our relationship to the next level."

Yep that line sent my heart beating a million times a second. I wanted to, but I couldn't. I didn't hide that from him and of course, he questioned it.

"Why can't you?" he asked.

I wanted to vomit thinking about why. I was not ready to share that part of my life with him. Yes, I wanted to move forward with him. So that meant I should have been able to talk to him about things right? Wrong! I was terribly afraid of his reaction.

"Things I can't change," I said.

He hit me another perfect line, "No one is perfect. We all have made mistakes. Done things we aren't proud of. It's okay. You don't have to tell me, but I do need to know will it affect us? I'm willing to move forward without knowing. That's just how much I care about you and trust you."

I could not lie to that man, "I do not know."

Tears began to flow, and he took me into his arms.

"Listen, we'll pray about it. Speak it out of existence," he said.

Lauren

A udrey did say she was willing to rebuild our friendship. She was genuinely honest. She and I began to do things together. It was good to have my friend back. We went out to lunch.

"Am I looking at our first lady?" I asked her.

Audrey laughed, " No ma'am!"

"So, what is going on then?"

She said she and pastor were taking things slow. She said he was a gentleman. I believed her. He was also good with Ariel. She loved him. He helped her with breathing treatments for her lungs. She absolutely loved when he drew or colored with her. What Audrey loved most was that he read her Bible stories and prayed with her.

"That is sweet. He will make a great stepdad or dad," I winked.

Audrey laughed, "I'm not listening to you."

I didn't want to bring it up, but I did, "Have you told him?"

She knew exactly what I was referring to. I was hoping that she told him before the town started to talk. I would hate for him to find out that way.

"No. I'm just not ready. He hasn't heard about it yet. Maybe the town will keep quiet," she said.

"You need to tell him before they talk!" I said.

"Promise me you won't tell him!" she said to me.

I assured her that I wouldn't tell him.

Pastor Reynolds

I was in my office at the church preparing for an upcoming sermon at a guest church. My youth pastor walked into my office.

"Pastor Adams how are you?" I greeted him.

"I'm fine Pastor, and yourself?"

"I'm great. What brings you by?"

He told me we needed to discuss some things. Some things that were not related to church affairs or business. I was interested in what we needed to talk about.

The discussion with Pastor Adams wasn't a good one. It was one that made me angry. I was so angry that I squeezed the steering wheel as I sped through the town to Audrey's apartment. I walked in and saw Ariel sitting at the kitchen table drawing. Audrey was cooking. She was excited to see me. She ran over to me and told me she tried a new dish that she wanted me to try. I ignored her.

"Ariel, can you go to your room and close your door for me? I need to talk to Mama."

When I heard the bedroom door close, I loosened my tie and placed my hands in my pants pockets. I eyed her. I wondered if she would tell the truth or if she would lie to me. After all, she hadn't really told me what was bothering her. I knew this was it.

"There was evidence that linked you as an accomplice to attempted murder. You got off because your brother lied for you. He's serving your time."

I watched as she broke down into tears. I really didn't care. That was something that you did not keep from someone you were building a relationship with.

"Let me explain," she cried.

"No! I gave you that opportunity! I asked you if it would affect us."

"You also said that we would pray it out of existence."

"I don't want to hear all that. We're done," I

said.

I left her apartment and headed home. I just started packing clothes. I didn't know where I was going. I knew I didn't want to be in Crestview. I just wanted to get out. Nobody knew I was leaving. My cell phone rang and rang as I drove out of the town. Audrey was calling. She was the last person I wanted to talk to. As I sped down the highway, dark clouds began to come in. There was a hotel in sight. I stopped and paid for a room. It was raining with frequent sounds of thunder. I turned the television on and threw myself onto the bed. I needed to clear my mind.

A news station interrupted the show with breaking news. I didn't want to hear no bad news. I had enough in my own life. I took the remote to turn off the television when I heard,

"One of the three tornadoes that were in the area has caused severe damage to Crestview."

Hail covered my windshield. It was very hard to see. Lightening flashed and thunder roared, but I managed to get back to the town. The welcome sign was torn down.

Trees filled the streets. Power lines were hanging. Houses that once stood were no longer there. Ambulances and fire trucks from surrounding cities were helping residents. The town hall was still standing. I couldn't drive to it. I parked my car and ran.

Almost every resident of Crestview was packed inside city hall. Rescue volunteers brought them there. Others fled there at the warning of the storm.

"Pastor R!" yelled Ariel, calling my name. I looked around for her. A fire-fighter was holding her. I rushed over to her and April.

"I want my Mama!" she cried.

Audrey was not with them. She was not in city hall. April didn't know where she was.

"She said she was going to your house, and she never came back! I thought she was with you," cried April.

"No, she's not," I said beginning to panic.

April burst into tears and fell to the floor, "I need my sister."

I pulled her up from the floor, "Stay with Ariel, I'm going to find her."

Both sides of the town were blocked with orange barricades. Police officers were not allowing anyone to enter the sides. They just didn't know that I was going through. They tried to stop me. I pushed through them all. There were no houses standing. No street signs. The only street sign left was the one I lived on. My house was completely destroyed. Debris was all I saw. I began to remove the debris. I found strength in me that I did not know I had. The only safe place in my house was my downstairs bathroom. I rushed to where my bathroom would have stood and began to lift the debris. Audrey's hand was there. Firefighters grabbed me and pulled me away.

"She's under there!" I yelled breaking away from them and running back to remove more debris.

"I can see her hand!"

The fire fighters helped me remove the debris. I cried at the sight of her lifeless body covered in dirt, bruises and scratches. I couldn't even remember the last time I cried. I took her into my arms.

"Sweetie, you have to wake up," I cried.

The firefighters stood around me. They were not moving. I knew what they were thinking. She was dead. An ambulance arrived. I picked her up and took her to it.

I stood next to the hospital bed. Audrey was not dead. Life support was helping her stay alive. I never imagined seeing her in that state. I never imagined anything happening like it had when I first arrived in Crestview. I kissed her on her wrapped forehead and left the room. The chapel was open. It was time for me to have a talk with God. I was telling everyone else to pray and trust in him while I forgot I needed to do the same.

Town workers were beginning to clean the streets. Residents were living in the town hall. Others lived in hotels outside of the town. Everything was destroyed. I drove to the church to see what was left. There was nothing.

Lauren

❧

"It was bound to happen," I said while walking up to Pastor Reynolds standing where the church once stood.

He turned to me and I thought about the promise I made to Audrey. I was about to break it. The church should have been destroyed. Temple of Heaven. What temple? It sure wasn't anything like Heaven. It was full of betrayal, guilt, lies and sin. All done by members, yet Audrey and I paid for it and lived with it.

"Audrey called me yesterday and told me you ended things with her because you had found out what happened." I said.

What Pastor Reynolds had told Audrey was not the truth. I left her years ago to face the town alone. I couldn't do it again. Everything happened right there where we stood. It was time for the truth to be left there.

"I have kept quiet for too long," I cried.

I told pastor what Audrey was too scared to tell him. My mother and her mother were best friends. It wasn't hard for him to conclude that the woman that sat on the 3rd row pew faithfully every Sunday was Audrey's mother. Everyone in town knew her as a successful real estate agent on the east side with two daughters that struggled to live on the west side. Yet, they chose to gossip about the lies. Her mother remarried when Audrey turned 18. She married Tameka's father who passed away years ago. Tameka never liked us in our teenage years. Things became worse when her father married Audrey's mom. She would try to tell us what really happened, but she didn't know the truth.

Audrey and I grew up in Temple of Heaven, baptized and all. We sang in the youth choir together. The youth pastor was over the choir. It happened to me first. We were 15 years old. After choir rehearsal, he would ask me to stay to practice a song. We would work on the song at the piano. When everyone was gone, he would take me to the storage room and rape me. I fought every time, but I never got away. Two years later, he left me alone and turned to Audrey. She was much tougher than I was. He started by saying little things to her. One day we were leaving rehearsal and I heard him ask her to stay. Before leaving the sanctuary, I remember seeing her standing at the piano as he began to play. The next day at school she told me what happened. I told her it had happened to me for two years. She wanted to tell, but I begged her not to. Audrey became pregnant by him. She told her mother. She said she didn't believe her. Audrey ran away to her brother. He came into town and beat the man so badly that he almost killed him.

Audrey had the baby. Her mother made her give it up for adoption. She knew Audrey was telling the truth.

April was a victim too. In her own home. By Tameka's father. She ran away to Audrey. She's been taking care of her sister ever since then.

"Who was the youth pastor then?" he asked me.

"He's still here. Walking around like he hasn't done a thing!"

"Pastor Adams," I said.

Pastor Reynolds

✾

The devil was definitely working through many people in that town. I became a victim of his misery. I listened to him myself. He stood in my office and toyed with my spirits. How did I let that happen? I wanted to get revenge, but that was not of God. Instead, I prayed and asked God to lift that weight from me.

The members of my church and myself were passing out food to residents in the town hall. We saw police officers walk in and over to Pastor Adams. I saw them place him in handcuffs. They were arresting him. Lauren then approached me.

"I had to do the right thing for Audrey," she

said.

I turned to her and said, "I'll be praying for your peace of mind, but yes you did the right thing."

Pastor Reynolds

A udrey was still in the hospital. I visited her every day. I prayed for her every day. I went to see her, and she was no longer on life support. Her head was still wrapped. She slightly opened her eyes. That was a miracle. I knew God was going to pull her through. She tried to talk. That was hard for her. I told her to rest. She lifted her hand and pointed at me. I assured her I was okay. I actually felt way better when she opened her yes.

The next day, April and Ariel went to see her. They were very happy to see her awake and recovering.

The houses were rebuilt. Among them were mine. I had my office back and I loved it. I was sitting at my desk working when my doorbell rang. I wasn't expecting anyone. I opened the door and there was Audrey. She had been discharged from the hospital. She didn't tell me; she wanted to surprise me. I was so happy to see her. We had so much to catch up on. I cooked dinner for us and we sat in my new kitchen, eating.

"I missed you," I said.

"I thought I had lost you that night. When you came to the hospital I was so happy."

I apologized for the way I acted, "I'm sorry for leaving like that. I should have let you explain the situation. Most of all I should've come in and talked to you about it."

"Lauren said you pulled me from the debris," she said.

Lauren had been a great blessing to me, because of her, I had a better understanding of Audrey. It was as if she was the guardian angel we both needed. I now understood why Audrey was a great mother. Her mother was not the best. She took care of her sister because she had always taken care of her.

She was reminded of the rape that day I played the piano at my house. The image she developed for pastors stopped her from allowing me in. I wasn't her predator. I was not trying to take from her. I wanted to give her all she deserved. She never wanted to talk about her childhood. It had a stronghold on her. She actually loved going to church at one point in time, but the sexual abuse turned her away.

Audrey

�֍

Daniel had figured me out. He was dead on with everything. My grandmother raised us. She took us to church. My mother started going later on when she met Tameka's father. She was an evil woman who only cared about herself. Drugs, men, beatings, beating us…we saw it all. Church was my escape. After the rapes, I felt different. Church was no longer my safe zone. My mother covered it all up with lies. She didn't want to ruin things with Tameka's father. A deacon of the church. She had the entire town believing that I lied about my age and slept with him. Lauren's mom made her keep quiet. Nobody believed me alone. "Well, there's a new church now. You should come," he said.

I knew what he was saying. All the sin and evil things that took place at the church was wiped away by the storm. He may have been right. I didn't know if I was ready to find out.

The next Sunday, I woke up and my apartment was empty. No April or Ariel. I figured Daniel picked them up and took them to church. He normally would. I decided I would get dressed and catch the bus to head to church.

Pastor Reynolds

❧

Audrey walked into the sanctuary of the church right before I gave the title of my sermon: "The Recipe of a Godly Woman" My sermon was derived from Proverbs 31:10-31, the virtuous woman. I first defined recipe as the necessary items a Godly woman has that pleases God. I then started my sermon. It had to let be known that man could not find or buy a virtuous woman because God shows her to him and will bring her to him. Any woman that God sent was worth more than any amount of money because she has value extended beyond any amount of money. A woman may claim to be a Godly woman, but will point her finger at other women she should be taking notes from. A Godly woman holds the heart of her husband so tough that she trusts her enough that he does not have to spoil her to keep her. A Godly woman does good by her husband until death separates them. She is true to wedding vows. A Godly woman is a hardworking woman and she isn't a selfish one. She is going to work hard to bring home the bacon and help those in need outside of her home. A woman of God is a strong, hard worker that is willing to reach out to help those in need. A woman of God is not worried about anything damaging her home. She knows God's grace and mercy will bring her family through anything. A Godly woman is royal, sent from the royal one Himself.

A woman of God can't just be in relations with any man, he has to be a man of God.

A Godly woman is not afraid to honor God.

She has the strength and faith in God to run the race and fight the battle until God calls her home.

She will then be able to rejoice in Heaven. A Godly woman is a wise woman. She is very kind with the personality of an angel. A

Godly woman is not focused on meaningless things because she has more important things to worry about, like her home. Godly women are known for saying, "I'm too blessed to be stressed."

A Godly woman does not entertain foolishness. She despises gossip and does not participate in it.

Most of all, a Godly woman knows how to stomp out the devil. A woman of God is a true mother to her children. She may not force them to come to church; but instead, she prays for them and gives them over to God.

A woman of God will receive praise from her children and husband because she is anointed.

Many women have done virtuous things, but those that remain virtuous is a virtuous woman.

A Godly woman is one of excellence. Many women can be deceiving, and their beauty could cause all kinds of mess if praised. That can be avoided by praising a true woman of God. A Godly woman can handle all things. She can overcome. She will stand through challenges. She will see her heavenly Father at the gates of Heaven.

Audrey

As Daniel interpreted the virtuous woman scripture, he had my attention. He was doing a great job. He continued his sermon by telling a story.

A Godly man was sent to a very small town. God told him to go preach His word. The man didn't ask questions such as: Was he going to like it? Who was he going to meet? How long was he going to be there?

He just said okay God and went. He told God he would do His will. The man began to preach at a church in the very small town. He met a woman. A beautiful woman. An intelligent woman. She was funny. She made him laugh. She made him smile. Most of all, she attended the church. She appeared to be a Godly woman. But she wasn't. It was all a front. She was a gossiper, meddled in other's business, and was spiteful. Satan tried to get him. The man still didn't ask questions. He continued to preach the word of God.

He met another woman. This woman was not like the last one. She had her guard up. The last one didn't. She wasn't as easy to get to like the last one. She also was beautiful. She also was intelligent. She was funny. She made him laugh. She made him smile. She didn't attend the church, but Satan was still showing up. He befriended the woman and Satan began to work a little harder.

This man became confused. He was lost. It was time to go to God. He asked God to show him and guide him, for he had lost sight in the women. God showed him a woman dressed in purple and silk. That woman was the one he befriended. God didn't have to tell the man how she was the Godly woman. God assured the man he knew. He just needed to tell the devil he was wrong and not feed in to him to fully step back into being the man of

God. The man told the devil he was wrong. God then sent him a vision. The woman wasn't perfect. She had a past. No man is perfect. We all have a past. We all have sinned, but the woman was trying to become a better person. She was working two jobs to care for her family. There was so much idleness going on around the town; yet, she kept her strength. She used her wisdom wisely. This woman also had a daughter that praised her. Why? She taught her daughter the one tool every person needs to make it in this world. She taught her daughter how to pray. A Godly woman has a deep relationship with God. She might not go to church all of the time, but she has a one of the kind relationship with God.

She was not afraid to call on him when things got rough. No matter where she was, she called on him.

One day, the man saw her praying outside of the library.

He ended the sermon by asking, "How many of you have prayed outside of a library?"

I tried to control my tears as everyone stood and clapped for him.

I couldn't. He had just preached a sermon about me.

Pastor Reynolds

🌿

A riel ran to me after church. I picked her up and hugged her. I didn't see her mother. I knew she was there. I spotted her standing in the back of the church inside of a pew. They headed her way. April joined them carrying her new born baby. She hugged her sister.

"Glad you came. Hope you stay for the second service."

I was glad she came too, "I hope she does stay," I said.

"I guess I can stay," sighed Audrey.

We headed to the fellowship hall. Dinner was being served after the service. I pulled out a chair for her to sit down. She sat down and went to get her food for her. I knew she was nervous and was not going to want to move much.

"I'm glad you stayed," I smiled, as I began to eat my food.

"Me too. I know it's a new church, but it actually feels like a new church" I said.

"Feels like when you used to attend?"

"Almost," I said.

I asked her, "Did you enjoy service?"

"I came in late. I heard your sermon. I'm saved. I know God. I try to live right. I have done some wrongs. Made some mistakes. I take care of my family…"

I cut her off, "A Godly woman. God showed you to me."

Audrey didn't respond to me. She took a sip of her water and sat it back down.

"I'm ready to be with you Audrey," I said to her.

"But….."

"But nothing. Come with me so we can talk," I said, while grabbing her hand. We got up from the table. I reached into my suit pants pocket and took out a black small box. When I opened the box, Audrey's mouth dropped as I kneeled down to ask her to marry me.

"You may not have the recipe of a Godly woman on your forehead, but you are. I love you Audrey. I want to be with you. I want to run this Christian race with you. I want to spend the rest of my life with you, but you have to be my wife. Will you marry me?"

Audrey smiled at me and said, "Yes, I will marry you."

About the Author

LaToya Geter-Shockley is a native of Little Rock, Arkansas. She is the daughter of the late Romunda Owens, who enjoyed reading her written work as a teenager. She attended the University of Arkansas at Pine Bluff where she obtained a Bachelor of Arts degree in Criminal Justice with a minor in Gerontology. She received her Master's degree in Human and Social Services from Walden University and is an active member of Sigma Gamma Rho Sorority, Inc. LaToya enjoys spending time with her husband, Marcus and their two dogs, Ace and Charlie. If not home cooking or playing video games, she can be found fishing, giving back to her community, or competing in pageants.

J. Kenkade
PUBLISHING®

Also Available from J. Kenkade Publishing

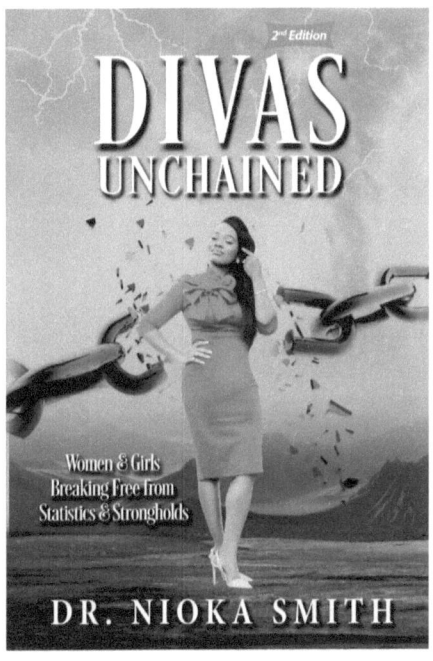

ISBN: 978-1-944486-25-9
Purchase at www.jkenkade.com or drniokasmith.com

The powerful chain-breaking reality of the many unfortunate strongholds our women and girls face and of one woman whose painful past almost killed her, until the voice of the Lord guided her into reversing Satan's plan. Dr. Nioka uses her divine gift to help women and girls break free from destructive life cycles and prosper in all areas of life. Discover what has been holding you back and take a journey as you see yourself within each turning page. Satan has lied to you. It's time to expose his lies. It's time to break free!

Also Available from
J. Kenkade Publishing

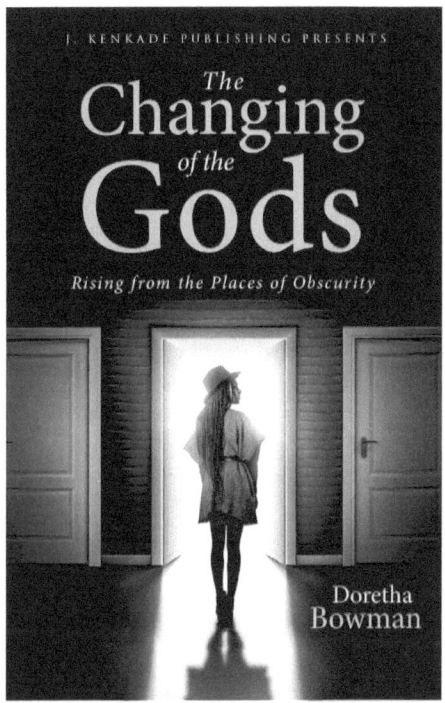

ISBN: 978-1-944486-26-6
Purchase at www.jkenkade.com

"The Changing of the Gods" describes one woman's life as it clung to the blind idolization of sin. From drug abuse, alcoholism, and victimization of sexual abuse, Doretha finds a way to make peace with her past through the aid of the guiding light of Christ, the true God. This book allows readers to acknowledge and rise from their places of obscurity to finally find the areas of their life that can be transformed by the light of Jesus Christ's salvation.